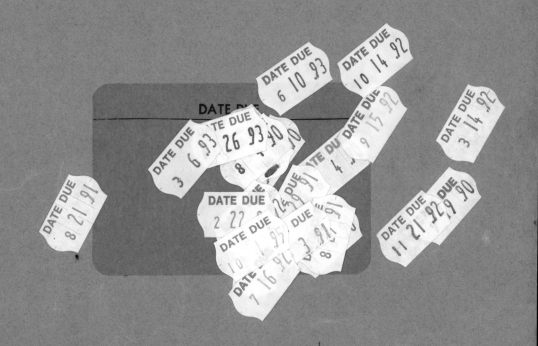

BABY IN THE BOX

Frank Asch

Holiday House / New York

To Charles, who likes boxes

Copyright © 1989 by Frank Asch
All rights reserved
Printed in the United States of America
First Edition

LIBRARY OF CONGRESS
Library of Congress Cataloging-in-Publication Data

Asch, Frank.
Baby in the box / written and illustrated by Frank Asch.
— 1st ed.
p.   cm.
Summary: Baby, a fox, and an ox play with blocks in a box.
ISBN 0-8234-0725-X
[1. Babies—Fiction.   2. Play—Fiction.   3. Stories in rhyme.]
I. Title.
PZ8.3.A7Bab   1989
[E]—dc19   88-16452   CIP   AC

ISBN 0-8234-0725-X

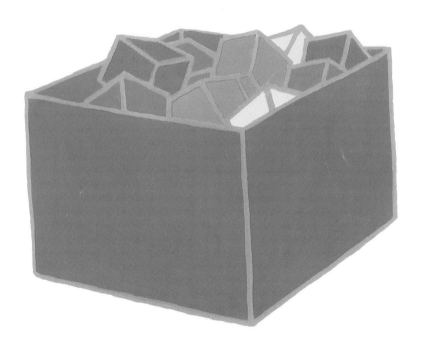

Blocks in the box.

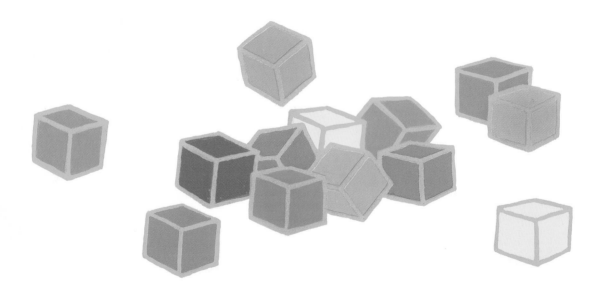

Blocks out of the box.

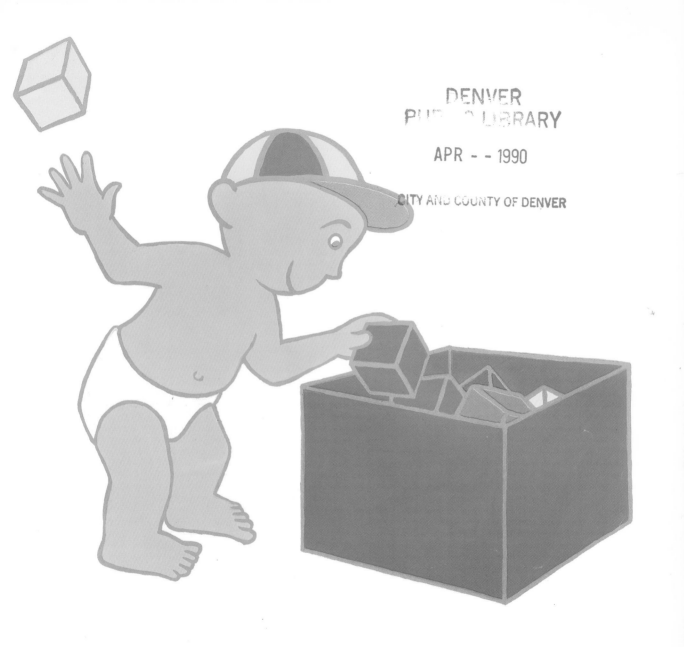

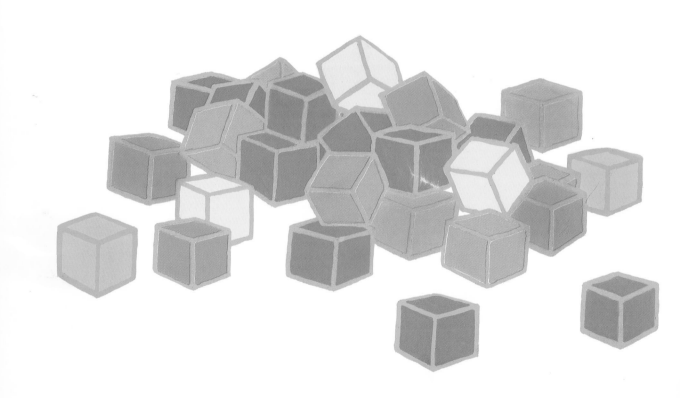

Baby in the box.

Fox.

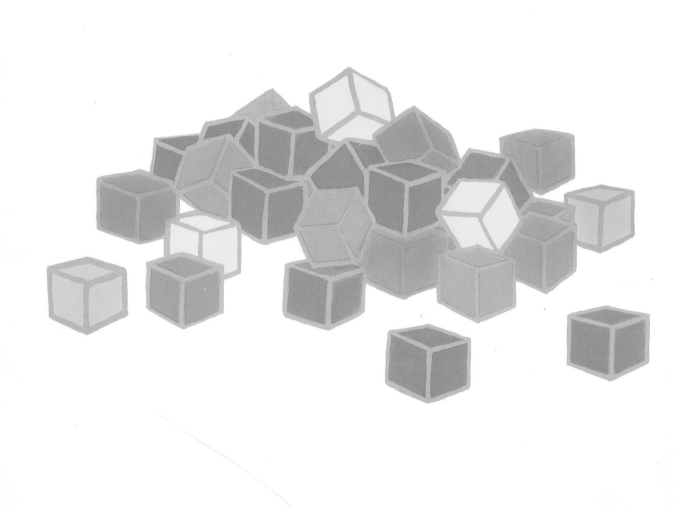

Baby and the fox in the box.

Baby and the fox

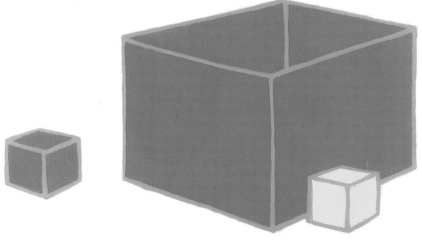

play with the blocks.

Ox.

Ox in the box.

Baby and the ox in the box.

Baby and the ox and the fox

in the box . . .

knock down the blocks.

"Time to clean up," says the ox.

"Time to go," says the fox.

Bye-bye, Fox. Bye-bye, Ox.

Bye-bye, Baby in the box.